The Lost Lady of Limone

The Lake Garda Mysteries

Volume 1

K.T. Ashbourne

ISBN: 1722016531
ISBN-13: 978-1722016531

DEDICATION

To Kim.

CONTENTS

ACKNOWLEDGMENTS

I would like to express my gratitude to the citizens of the ports around Lake Garda for their patience and kindness.

1 THE NEWCOMER

When the aircraft flew low over Verona, Kim saw a brief but quite spectacular view of the city; she could even make out its famous lofty tower loitering in the air high above the square. The plane glided smoothly into land with a reassuring but startling bump as the wheels made contact with terra firma. The passengers breathed an audible, collective sigh of relief.

As Kim stepped out of the plane and onto the stairway she was immediately stunned by the sheer temperature of the air, and the blazing brightness of the sun. It all took her breath away. She trooped after the crowd and made her way into the terminal.

After she had queued for what seemed like an interminable duration, but was in fact only eight minutes, Kim cleared passport control. Evidently she was welcome in Italy. The guard had said so.

Kim peered down the baggage reclaim steps and spotted the staff member sent to greet her. This was not what she'd signed up for. She thought that by now she would have been skiing down the Austrian Alps, having fun with a crowd of young holiday makers. And now here she was covering a post in Verona, the favourite holiday place for the over seventies.

She came down the stairs with a heavy heart.

"You Kim?" enquired the hideously ugly youth, with an air

of complete indifference. His scrawny frame barely filled the staff uniform.

"I suppose I am" Kim muttered.

"Griff" he uttered.

"What?" yelled Kim. "What did you say to me?"

"Griff" he repeated. "G R I F F me Griff, you Kim" he explained.

"You poor sod" mumbled Kim thoughtlessly. "I mean, thanks for meeting me."

"That's okay" he managed to utter.

"Griff, that's a Welsh name, isn't it?" Kim enquired.

"Sort of. Parents had a caravan in Wales" he explained.

"I don't quite follow" she replied.

"I was conceived in Wales. Gave me a Welsh name. Just didn't know how to spell it" he expanded.

"You poor sod" laughed Kim.

"Ugh. Car's this way" and he led her to a rusty Fiat 500, which, dating from its appearance, looked as if it had been assembled in 1760.

The vehicle snarled as it crawled onto the highway.

"Is it far to the office, or base hotel, or whatever?" asked Kim sweetly.

"Garda. Bloody miles" he murmured.

Kim slumped into a deep depression. Garda. Playground

of the over nineties. She sighed, and thought, well, only for a couple of weeks. She'd survive. At least, as long as the old dears don't start conking out on her.

*****

"Welcome, welcome! Now Kim, I'm Sara the team leader, any questions at all, just ask me and I'll tell you where to go. And any complaints, let me know and I'll tell you where to go with them too! Just my little joke. You are allocated to this hotel as your base, and this list of other hotels too". She handed over a wad of papers. "This constitutes your staff welcome pack, and this is the customer welcome pack". Another great wad of paper was dumped onto her. "Any suggestions, improvements, new ideas, anything at all, let me know, and I'll tell you where to go. Got it?" Sara enquired, clearly expecting no response.

"Just one question" ventured Kim, glancing around the deserted hotel lobby. It had seen better days, but then thought Kim, maybe it would look more presentable in the morning sun. Nowhere looks appealing at half two in the middle of the night, especially when you're exhausted.

"Any chance of a cuppa? I'm gasping."

"Griff, tea for three" commanded Sara.

Griff sauntered out with a barely audible "Ugh".

Shortly he stumbled back with a tray laden with tea and small cakes. He slumped into one of the chairs and gazed out of the window at the occasional passing traffic.

"Surname?" queried Sara.

"Tomlinson" answered Kim, "same spelling as Tomlinson Holidays and Tomlinson Airways."

"Really?" asked Sara.

"Yes. Father's very proud of his business, but insists I earn my way up the ladder by learning every aspect of the business from the ground floor up" Kim announced in a matter of fact voice.

"Really?" Sara gasped.

"No way!" grumbled Griff. "Any chance of a pay rise?"

"Well, we'll soon get you shaped up, we'll do you proud!" gushed Sara. She shuffled her papers nervously.

"Tomorrow you can follow on with the tourists on a walking tour of the old centre of Garda, and listen carefully, as you'll be doing it in the afternoon. So pay attention to the route, and all the relevant stories. In any case, both the route and the script are detailed in your staff pack" Sara excitedly proclaimed.

She certainly knew how to get a girl really enthused thought Kim.

"Okay, team leader, what time?" she asked.

"Ten sharp, here in the lobby. Your converted basement store room is unfortunately flooded, so temporarily you've been placed in an empty suite. Don't get used to it" Sara sternly warned.

"Fine. Tired. Going to bed now. Night" and Kim followed Sara as indicated.

"Hey, breakfast at eight, staff kitchen!" called Griff as Kim slipped into the elevator.

Kim entered her suite, and without even taking in her luxury surroundings, lay on the bed, and fell asleep.

*****

A phone call in the morning dragged her out of her slumbers. This was an unwarranted cruelty for which she was ill prepared. Surely this was a breach of human rights?

"Breakfast" announced Griff.

It was Kim's turn to reply "Ugh".

She dropped the phone and staggered into the bathroom, eventually noticing the elegant suite she was occupying.

*****

Having blundered around the hotel for twenty minutes, and being misdirected several times by an indifferent hotel staff, she finally stumbled into her intended destination. In the staff kitchen she soon found Griff and joined him at the plain table in the even plainer room. He nodded good morning, and showed her where to get her breakfast. After a few minutes an elderly Italian gentleman appeared.

"Miss Tomlinson?" he enquired. Griff pointed at her.

"That's me!" chirped Kim.

"May I wish you a warm welcome to our hotel!" gushed the man.

"My name is Carlos, I am the hotel manager, and anything you need, please just ask".

"Thanks, that's great!" responded Kim, delighted.

"And of course you may use the luxury suite for as long as you need it, entirely at our pleasure" added the manager.

"Well, thank you so much, that means a great deal to me, really, terrific!" Kim smiled sweetly, desperately suppressing a giggle.

"I bid you good day, ciao!" and he went about his business.

Griff eyed her at length.

"So you're dead rich then? With daddy's money" he uttered.

"Not exactly. I wouldn't say that" Kim replied nonchalantly.

"What then?" enquired Griff.

"Well, as my father owns Tomlinson Fish and Chips in Stretford, Manchester, I suppose he is a man of property, but not really all that rich" Kim explained silkily.

"A chip shop? You said he owned the whole airline!"

"Oh, no, I said he was proud of his business. Sara just assumed I meant the airline and holiday company" Kim smiled so sweetly.

Griff roared with laughter. "You cheeky little minx! Absolutely bloody brilliant! Now you've got that Sara running around like a headless chicken! Superb!" and Griff laughed again.

"You won't let on, will you?" Kim pleaded.

"Too bloody true I won't, this going to be so good,

watching her crawl up to you on a daily basis. Brilliant!" Griff chuckled. "Anyway, see you in the lobby at ten, you wretched impostor! Outstanding!" and he went on his way, chortling aloud.

*****

2 GARDA

A large group of assorted persons, many of whom were in fact under the age of ninety, milled aimlessly around the hotel lobby. Griff was attempting to install a modest measure of order, but to little avail. Kim sighed as she cast her weary eyes over the motley throng. They can be an unruly lot, these nonagenarians, she concluded.

"Right!" she yelled. "Form up in good order!"

And to Griff's amazement, they obeyed. Griff waited for further instructions to emerge, but none were issued.

"So what now? whispered Griff.

"How should I know? It's your show" responded Kim.

"Okay, right" he muttered, then in the best voice he could command "now all of you follow me, I am your leader!"

"Good morning leader" they all merrily chirped, and ambled out of the hotel and into the bright sunlight of a beautiful Italian morning.

The group stumbled along the rough narrow lanes, following Griff's lead, as he pointed out a startling variety of buildings of architectural merit. Griff recited the prepared points of interest and fascinating stories of long ago as per the mandatory schedule. Kim observed that the crowd of enthusiastic octogenarians loved it, for by now, she had realized that they couldn't be quite so ancient after all. Great, she thought, it'll be my turn soon, with the next lot of sorry coffin dodgers, and she chuckled to herself, but she did note all the relevant anecdotes.

The excited gaggle of humanity shuffled steadily along the narrow streets, gaining insights into the follies and triumphs of the past, and honing their wisdom as they progressed. They turned a sharp corner, and emerged into a small square on the lake shore. They all stopped to absorb the view. Kim edged her way to the front of the throng, and not too gently at that. She took her first look at the lake, the sun glistening on the delicate ripples dancing on the lake, the surrounding hills, resplendent in their foliage and blossom, the quaint cafes and shops, blazing white, and the distant shoreline shimmering in the haze. She was struck speechless by the beauty of the scene, and her dazzled eyes darted this way and that, the better to soak in the extraordinary spectacle.

She felt her mood lighten and lift, and it occurred to her that maybe, just maybe, she had struck lucky in being posted here.

*****

The stroll along the shoreline was delightful, but the merry company waned somewhat in the heat, so all were happy when Griff announced that the tour would end in the next square with a glass of wine or juice, provided by a local worthy merchant. Kim headed for the wine table; Griff redirected her to the juice.

"Booze strictly for the punters" he explained.

"Bloody typical" complained Kim, sipping an orange juice.

"Never mind. I'll get you a crate of lager back at the

Ranch" enthused Griff.

"Ranch?" asked Kim.

"Local office. Sara's joint. We meet tonight at seven. Get orders or marching orders – you know. Take you there myself later" Griff offered.

"Thanks – I think" mumbled Kim.

*****

In the afternoon it was Kim's duty to lead an amiable cluster of quite innocent holidaymakers, who had duly assembled in the lobby of a nearby hotel, the Bella Vista. This rather down market hotel boasted a grand view of the local bus station. Griff followed her, as both mentor and inspector, to ensure she kept to the authorized route and script. She marched her group in good order and pace as she recounted the horrors and delights of bygone years, not exactly echoing Griff's delivery, but rather enhanced and embellished with gory or sumptuous detail as she thought appropriate. When they rounded a sharp corner, she quite forgot the associated anecdote, but since romance at short notice had always been her forte, she strove to entertain the throng with a contrivance, not merely of incidental embellishment, but of sheer fabrication.

She told of how the noble Grand Duke had promised his only daughter to the local count, a gruesome old villain who had already gone through two previous wives – in suspicious circumstances - and how she had to be physically forced at sword point into the blessed estate of holy matrimony. Though, as time passed, and she mellowed, she fell hopelessly, madly in love. But not with the decrepit count, no, but with his beautiful younger sister. The two illicit lovers then engaged in a raging affair that lasted for many years, and there was nothing the count could do – was there? – for he could not return his faithless bride on that score – could he?

The mob loved it. Griff hid his face. Kim glared at him triumphantly.

Later, upon completion of the tour, Griff tackled her on the question of historical accuracy.

"Look, Kim, you just can't make it up, you know" Griff objected with an appeal to reason but with a noticeable lack of conviction.

"Course I can!" cried Kim. "I can make it up pretty darn good! The crowd loved it! They're on holiday, not a lecture tour, if they want real history, they can study dull books in their local library – they're here for fun, and I gave it them good and proper!"

Griff grinned. "You're going to be a right handful! What the hell am I going to tell Sara?"

"Tell her the truth! That I was absolutely terrific!" Kim answered.

*****

At seven o'clock sharp the entire crew gathered in Sara's office. It was a shambolic room above a busy laundry which emitted an aroma that defied description. Kim glanced around her grim surroundings. The usual office clutter of laptops, faxes and photocopiers were present, and shelving groaning under the weight of reams of documents inviting their readers to book expensive tours to amazing localities of fantastic interest both near and far. Kim was astonished to learn that Rome, Naples and Venice were just a mere hop down the road.

Sara called the meeting to order, and the group took uncomfortable chairs around a battered central table.

"Right, everyone" she began. "This is Kim, new girl, posted for a while. I have to warn you she is the daughter of Lord Tomlinson, Group Chairman, so best behaviour please. We don't want any ill reports making their way back, do we?"

The team regarded Kim with renewed interest and more than a little suspicion. Kim drew herself up and tried to look important.

Sara introduced the others.

"Griff you know already, Rachel has been here the longest, so you can ask her anything about the resorts, and Alice is also a pretty recent starter too, but is already an expert on the local bars and cafes".

Alice laughed. "Hey, I like prosecco, so what else is a girl to do?"

"You're not supposed to drink in public bars where the punters can see you" explained Griff. "Gives the wrong impression".

"Exactly so" reinforced Sara.

Griff reached below the table, and dragged over a crate of lager.

"Course we can all have a drop in here" he ventured,

handing bottles round.

The remainder of the meeting consisted of verbal reports, and Sara issued schedules of pick up and drop off times and targets for bookings. Kim paid scant attention. Dull stuff was not her strong point. The lager was welcome though.

"So how did Kim do this afternoon?" Sara enquired loudly. Kim snapped out of her reverie.

"Did bloody good!" assured Griff. "Bloody good, for a fact!"

"Glad to hear it" Sara replied. "Meeting over" she added.

3 A FAMILY REUNION

Kim regarded the herd of elderly tourists assembled in the hotel lobby with something akin to a predator eyeing up its prey. From her clipboard she called out the roster of volunteers. They duly answered as present and correct. A final tardy couple emerged from the lift.

"Mr. and Mrs. Ackroyd" hollered the man.

"Arthur and Gladys" responded Kim, and she checked them off her list.

"It's Mrs. Ackroyd to you" snapped Mrs. Ackroyd sharply. "So don't you presume to take liberties without invitation" she added coldly.

"Oh, sorry" muttered Kim, and she turned to address the assembly.

"Right!" she yelled abruptly. "Walking frames at the ready – let's get clanking down the road!"

She led the startled posse into the blazing sunshine at a brisk canter. They all advanced smartly along the prescribed route.

She enunciated the requisite script, but only up to a certain point. She engaged in some light banter with her charges, but was careful to be very respectful to Mrs. Ackroyd. Eventually there was the inevitable moment when boredom struck home. Kim was now in her element.

They veered around a sharp bend, and halted to view the beautiful, narrow cobbled lane, lined with attractive blossom draped cottages, and quaint houses adorned with architectural features. A few small villas boasting well attended gardens added charm to the spectacle.

"In this garden" began Kim in an authoritative voice, "a particularly fractious family dispute resulted in three corpses being buried under the shrubs" and she indicated the spot.

"And even to this day you can see the result in the vibrant bougainvillea with its vivid scarlet hue – a permanent memorial to the unfortunates thereunder" she added with a dramatic flourish.

She carried on in this vein along the whole length of the street; no property was spared.

The holidaymakers learned of how an unrequited guest who overstayed his welcome had been hurled from a lofty rooftop. Two greedy cousins had been hung from a branch, one at either end of the same rope, to see which one was the heavier. Neither survived the experiment. A disobedient servant had been beheaded on a Sunday morning – the easier that his soul may enter heaven. Kim warmed to her theme.

"In this house lived two twins – brothers – who developed the game of waking each other every day by a stab in the leg with a small knife. They were called the stabbing twins" Kim explained.

"Have you ever heard the phrase 'stabbing twins' anyone?" she enquired.

No one could admit to ever having heard the expression. But that was no surprise, as it was conceived and cultivated quite recently in her fertile imagination.

"But one day, a fatal blow was struck, and in consequence the culprit duly executed. And that was the end of the stabbing twins!" she bellowed.

By the time the exhausted crowd had reached the ultimate square, hot, thirsty and emotionally traumatized, not only did they quaff the proffered wine, but downed large gins besides. The delighted worthy merchant rewarded Kim with a triple strawberry gelato.

'A treat well earned' mused Kim 'for such bloodthirsty exertions'.

*****

Kim lounged on her bed, relishing the luxury of her suite. She felt not one jot of guilt. After all, she had not asked for a free luxury room – the hotel had advanced it, presumably as some sort of bribe for their principal customer's daughter. What was she to do but enjoy? Why entertain qualms when a wonderful view over the lake was to be appreciated from her balcony. She rose, and sauntered over to open the door and gazed out over the waters. As she leant on the balustrade and absorbed the excellent view it seemed to her that life could be pretty good.

A knock on the door gained her attention. The hotel manager appeared somewhat agitated.

"Hi," welcomed Kim "anything up?" she queried.

"Well" began the manager, "I have a friend" and he hesitated..."who has a vineyard".

"Brilliant!" enthused Kim.

"He would like to supply Tomlinson Airlines, and wondered if you could recommend his produce?" the manager explained.

"Me?" asked Kim. "I know precious little about wine" she volunteered.

"Perhaps I can educate your palette, with a sample of dry prosecco, medium and rose also. Do you think that might be possible?" he wondered with a disingenuous air.

"I suppose" replied Kim.

"Wonderful" and he snapped his fingers.

A waiter advanced from the corridor and pushed a hand truck into the room. It was bearing three crates of wine, one crate each of dry, medium and rose prosecco.

"Please to try each, and recommend any or all to the airline. I thank you" and the manager bowed and was gone.

Once the door was closed, and footsteps could no longer be heard, Kim screeched with delight.

"This is stonking!" she yelped aloud.

"Can things get any better?" she added as she whirled in sheer joy around her ill-gotten gains.

*****

Griff aided and abetted the transfer of the loot from her room to the Ranch. His ailing Fiat 500 fairly groaned under the load. Griff hauled the treasure up the stairs, one crate at a time. They slid the trove under the table.

"Thanks mate, couldn't have done it without you" Kim admitted.

"Sure thing" acknowledged Griff.

The others arrived and Sara called the meeting to order.

The usual meeting droned on in the usual way, until Sara reprimanded Kim.

"Kim. Your highlights of historical dramas and so on. Too gory. You'll have to tone it down a bit. Had complaints. Punters like a bit of gore, but not so much they have nightmares. Okay, got it?" Sara advised.

"Okay, got it, wilco" Kim stated sheepishly.

Griff started grinning at her. If he'd have done that he'd have bloody well been fired; good job Sara still thought she was a Tomlinson Royal.

"Meeting over" pronounced Sara.

"I could murder a prosecco…." Alice cried wistfully.

"As it happens" Kim responded, and she shoved a crate forward with her feet.

Alice nearly fainted with delight. She set to will a will. And she carried on setting to for some time. For each sip the others consumed, Alice downed a glass.

Finally she announced in a loud voice "It's getting too hot in here!" and she proceeded to shed a garment. They all laughed, save Griff, who paid close attention as another garment was cast aside.

"Hey!" yelled Sara – "We'd better get her home" and they contrived to restore a modicum of decency as Alice firmly resisted their efforts. Griff sat back and enjoyed the spectacle.

They helped her outside but once in the fresh air it was clear from her stagger that she would not get far.

"Take her to my place, it's nearest, and Luciano won't mind" Rachel suggested.

Sara and Kim assisted Rachel in steering the heavy maiden in the requisite direction, until they reached the apartment, and while Rachel fumbled with her keys to open the door Sara and Kim propped their colleague against the wall, and between them balanced her.

Eventually they got her inside and dumped her on the couch. She flopped down with a mighty thud.

"Your boyfriend going to be okay with this?" asked Sara.

"No problem" reassured Rachel.

"Thanks, Rachel, nice one" muttered Sara, as the two departed the scene.

"So next time, maybe just one bottle, not a whole crate, okay?" Sara stated as they made their way along the street.

"Agreed" smiled Kim, "definitely agreed".

*****

Some days later Kim was indulging in a siesta in her room, when the phone rang. It was Sara.

"Got a wonderful surprise for you!" Kim heard. "Your father is here, I'll bring him straight up!" and the line went dead.

Kim was completely startled. She thought her mum and dad had gone to Majorca for two weeks. What could her dad be doing here? – must be terrible news!

A knock at the door brought her to steel herself for the worst. She opened it tentatively. Sara marched in. A handsome man, aged about fifty five, tall, slim but with greying hair, and sporting a very sharp suit, trooped in behind her.

"Look, Lord Tomlinson – your daughter – working here as I said!" she exclaimed. "So I guess I'd better leave you two to it, you must have a lot of catching up to do!" and she excused herself and left, closing the door behind her.

Kim stared at the peer of the realm.

The peer of the realm stared at Kim.

"You know," he began "I honestly think that if I hadn't been told for a fact that you were my daughter, I don't believe I would have recognized you. You appear to have lost six years in age, six pounds in weight, but gained six inches in height. The Italian sunshine, diet and lifestyle must suit you perfectly. It really is a remarkable transformation" and he waited for a response.

"Well" blurted out Kim "I'm not exactly your daughter, you see".

"Indeed? Then pray tell who you are - exactly" he demanded.

"Well, you see, I may not be your daughter, exactly, but I am a Tomlinson – Kim Tomlinson – to be precise" She explained.

"Oh, do go on, I so relish precision" added the earl.

"So I said that I worked in my father's business, which I

did, and they all assumed I was your daughter – so I let them carry on assuming it because I got this great room and lots of free coffees instead of some horrid crash pad like the others, you see..." she rambled.

"I understand, and quite precisely at that" he interrupted. "It's called pecuniary advantage by deception, and I'll have no part of it" he announced very clearly.

"Oh" said Kim. "You see, my dad has his own business too, it's the second largest fish and chip shop in Stretford, and it's the only one that will serve gravy with fish and chips, when I'm on I always give an extra large portion of gravy if people want it on their fish – it's a Stretford speciality – so I indulge them. Dad says the customer is always right" Kim gushed.

"Quite so," agreed the Chairman of the Group "quite so. And here you have developed your own little gravy train, I surmise".

"Well, I'm not going to say no, am I? If the hotel wants to give me their best room in order to bribe your family, and all that booze too, well, why not? No cost to the company, is it?" Kim ventured.

"No cash cost, just a reputational nightmare" he replied. "Although I had heard you quite generously shared the booze so sinisterly acquired. At least that much can be said for you".

Before Kim could respond, the hotel phone rang. She wrestled it off its stand. It was Sara again. "His Lordship's car is here. I'll come up for him" she added bluntly.

Kim turned to her erstwhile father. "Your car's here. Sara's coming for you. You won't tell, will you?" she pleaded.

"I will not participate in any deception, of any kind" he replied.

There was an awkward silence, which seemed to be interminable. A knock at the door, and Kim opened it dreading the next words spoken.

"Car's here" Sara stated.

"Thank you" and he turned to face her. "Now Sara, I don't want you to think of Kim here as my daughter, but just as any other ordinary employee, no special privileges, no perks, no easy roster duties, or anything of that sort. Just treat her as a regular employee, and put it completely out of your mind that she is any relative of mine at all. I trust that is clear" he intoned emphatically.

"Clear as a bell!" she chimed, and smiled sweetly at Kim.

He turned to regard Kim once more.

"And as for you, young lady, may I wish you every success with your present endeavours, adieu!" and he swirled out of the room.

Kim breathed a sigh of relief and crashed onto the bed.

*****

4 VERONA

Kim took the next group out on the walking tour around Garda. Keep it toned down, she reminded herself. As they rounded the corner to her favourite little lane, she spotted that posies of flowers had been left at the point of the supposed graves. She resolved not to repeat that particular anecdote. Don't want the locals getting alarmed or suspicious.

But a new story manifested itself - it just emerged from the depths of her imagination. Kim blurted it out, even as it surfaced into her consciousness.

"Now this quaint abode features a deep cellar - ostensibly for storing wine and olive oil" she started. Once she was in her stride, there was no holding her back.

"But a passing English vicar was abducted right on this very spot, here," she pointed to the cobbled pavement in a dramatic gesture, "and cast into the infernal darkness of that dreadful cellar" she proclaimed with attendant menace.

"Then those merciless miscreants wrote to the Pope asking him what to do with their protestant captive. But the Pope thought it was a joke, and didn't reply, the year then being nineteen ten" she paused for effect.

"Eventually the parish priest heard what they'd done, and after a mere three and a half months the unfortunate was released. The half starved cleric had lost five stone, his bleached skin stretched over his scrawny carcass, his hair had gone quite grey, and upon release he promptly left Italy never to return. He didn't even pay for his board and lodging – three and half months for free!" and she chortled with glee.

The defenceless entourage was subjected to further anecdotes of brazen brutality but doubtful authenticity as they obediently trooped after her. They were only too relieved when Kim announced that the tour was ending with refreshments. They took their selection of drinks and slumped into the available chairs, fanning themselves in the heat and thanking their great fortune in being alive now and not in times past.

*****

Rachel grabbed Kim in the hotel lobby. "Hey, I'm free this afternoon, and you are too. I'm going into Verona for a change, want to come along?"

"Okay, great, where shall we meet up?" Kim enquired.

"Old bus station, one o'clock sharp" and Rachel was gone.

*****

Kim waited patiently at the due time, and Rachel emerged from a side street. They made their way to the ticket office, and a torrent of Italian burst forth from Rachel's lips. Kim stared, amazed. An equal torrent erupted from the lady in the ticket office, and tickets and cash were duly exchanged.

"You follow that?" Rachel teased.

"Not a syllable" admitted Kim.

"That's fine. Once you've been here five years like me,

you'll get to pick it up" she encouraged.

"I guess it helps living with an Italian boyfriend" suggested Kim.

"Well, there is that, true, though there are times we just don't get a chance to talk at all" quipped Rachel.

Kim giggled, and they chatted merrily on the slow but relaxing bus ride to Verona.

As they ambled around Rachel introduced the key attractions of the famous city to Kim. They took selfies beneath Juliet's balcony, but skipped the ritual of leaving an eternal padlock fixed to the nearby fencing in the courtyard. Kim admitted to feeling entirely dizzy at the summit of the old tower.

"Never thought I'd get vertigo in Verona!" she admitted, "But it is a fabulous view".

Rachel smiled "Time for a coffee and cake" and she led Kim to the central square café below, where a table was luckily available.

"Latte" ordered Kim when the waiter finally appeared.

"Café latte" corrected Rachel "or all you will get is milk. One for me too she added" and the waiter noted the order, including a selection of cakes, and then he strolled off to clear another table apparently having forgotten them already.

A few minutes later a familiar couple approached the café, and Kim hid her face.

"What's wrong?" asked Rachel.

"Punters. Two o'clock" answered Kim in a whisper.

"They're everywhere, you get used to it" Rachel reassured her.

"But these two – I mean he's okay, but she's a right dragon!" Kim intimated.

The couple spotted a vacant table next to the two colleagues, and scurried to claim it. Once they were settled in their seats, they looked around to take in their surroundings, and to try to attract a waiter.

"Hello there!" called Mr. Ackroyd "Good afternoon" added Mrs. Ackroyd coldly.

"Hello, good afternoon" replied Kim. "Enjoying the sights?" she queried.

"I should say so!" he responded.

"Entirely charming" added his wife.

The newcomers ordered their drinks, and a after a brief chat among themselves, Mr. Ackroyd held forth once more.

"It's certainly different from Milton Keynes" be began.

"Really?" answered Rachel, coming to Kim's aid.

"Though we won't be there after this holiday" he added.

"No indeed" joined Mrs. Ackroyd "we sold our home there, and have purchased a bungalow in Bournemouth. It's being renovated now, and when we return we shall start our retirement together in our new abode".

"Brilliant!" responded Kim.

"It's barely five hundred yards from the beach" boasted

Mr. Ackroyd.

"It sounds wonderful" rejoined Rachel.

"And we shall join the local church to cultivate a new circle of friends, as at present we know no one in Bournemouth" Mrs. Ackroyd explained.

"Sounds like a plan" Kim uttered.

"In a couple of days we're going to visit Limone" Mr. Ackroyd continued "we booked that trip for sure".

"I'm on that one in a couple of days – maybe I'll be your guide!" Kim enthused but winced at the thought.

"Mr. Ackroyd has outdone himself – he bought me a new lemon hat, lemon dress, shoes and bag – all lemon for the trip to Limone" volunteered Mrs. Ackroyd.

"Nothing's too good for you, Gladys" Mr. Ackroyd stated.

"It's the first time in decades he's bought me anything of the sort – and I admit I would not have selected such a garish combination myself – but I daresay I'll wear it, if only the once" Mrs. Ackroyd remarked.

"Well I'll see it all in a couple of days then" Kim said.

"Well, we wish you both a long and comfortable retirement" added Rachel, closing the conversation. She then rose, and the two girls fled the scene.

They strolled round a little more, and did some desultory shopping, mainly looking and not buying, before deciding the hour was getting late, and it was time to return to Garda.

Kim nodded off on the bus ride home, and once they had

alighted she apologized for being such poor company.

"Not at all" cried Rachel, "best day off in yonks" and they hugged and went their separate ways.

*****

5 SVETLANA

The usual meeting droned on in the Ranch. After all the routine points and assignments had been made, Sara admonished Kim once more.

"Kim, tales, gore, nightmares, desist. Got it?" she snapped.

"Got it" accepted Kim, feeling downhearted. It was her one bit of real fun.

"And one other item, our regional manager Svetlana will be arriving shortly, to review our paperwork, she says, but I'm sure it's to meet Kim, in reality" Sara observed.

"Meeting over" she concluded abruptly.

They had a very modest sip of prosecco each, and tidied around somewhat. At least the table and window sill were clear, so it gave a general impression of order.

As Kim was shuffling a wad of papers into shape, Griff approached her, and very quietly said to her "If that Svetlana asks you back to her villa, skip it".

He retreated before she could respond.

Later Alice sidled up to her as she arranged files on the shelves. "Little tip for you - that Svetlana – she's alright really – but don't get roped into any sightseeing round her villa".

"Okay, right, thanks for the tip" Kim replied.

By now Kim's curiosity was arising. What was it about this villa that had caught their attention?

Rachel took her opportunity while Kim was within close earshot.

"Word to the wise, Svetlana's villa – give it a miss if an invite is chucked your way" she whispered mysteriously.

"Right – wilco" Kim responded.

Now Kim really was wondering what marvels or dreads this villa contained. She was bursting to ask, but the general conversation covered every topic but this one.

Finally Sara caught her attention for a brief quiet word.

"It's a fair bet Svetlana will ask you to go see her Villa. Best bet for you is to say – thanks, but no thanks – got it?" and she said more on the subject.

Right – that was it! If Svetlana so much as hinted at a villa trip Kim would grab it like a flash!

In due course Svetlana arrived. She swirled into the office with a flourish.

Sara made the requisite introductions. Svetlana merely smiled politely.

Kim regarded her with close attention. Svetlana was in her late thirties, maybe even early forties, hard to tell which. She was very elegantly dressed, tall, slim, and had blonde hair framing a most beautiful face. Her skin had an immaculate peaches and cream complexion. She floated around the room with a grace that Kim envied, and did not so much stand at the photocopier, as pose beside it. As she sat on a chair, she did not slump down, but adopted an upright posture which then morphed into another elegant pose. Kim stared at her, both fascinated and envious.

Finally Svetlana addressed Kim in a strained foreign accent. "So, Kim, how is your Italian?"

"Just starting to learn it" admitted Kim.

"I see. What other languages do you command?" Svetlana sweetly enquired.

"Well, only English, really" Kim replied.

Svetlana regarded her at some length.

"I am fluent in German, Italian, English, French and of course Polish, and I have working knowledge of Russian, Spanish, Czech and Serbo-Croat" she coldly informed.

"This is Europe" she added.

"Oh" Kim responded.

"This is why I am regional manager, and you are chalet girl" Svetlana asserted.

"Well yes" Kim vaguely replied.

"You did apply to be chalet girl in Austria, yes?" Svetlana asked.

"Well, I did, but I'm glad I got sent here instead" Kim feebly answered.

"I am surprised Lord Tomlinson has not driven you harder, but he is such a nice man, I suppose" Svetlana ventured.

"Yes, very nice" Kim trembled.

Kim relaxed as Svetlana's attention turned elsewhere.

After spending fifteen minutes reviewing the details of office reports and other routine items, Svetlana approached Kim.

"How would you like a ride out to see my beautiful villa in its rolling landscape? See some of the real Italy. Maybe learn three words of Italian" she invited at last.

"Love to!" exclaimed Kim thoughtlessly.

"Wonderful! I pick you at eight tomorrow! Bring your bikini for the pool!" Svetlana enthused.

"Your husband won't mind?" Kim asked.

"I have no husband – no man will ever own me!" and Svetlana smiled as she waved at the others and vanished with a final flourish.

*****

Kim waited impatiently in the hotel car park. An Alfa Romeo convertible swept into sight, revealing Svetlana at the wheel, looking simply amazing. Kim groaned with jealousy.

"Your ride, miss" and Svetlana swung the door open.

"Thanks" chirped Kim as she climbed in.

They screeched through the town streets at an outrageous speed, and careered along the country highways even faster. Svetlana drives worse than most Italians, thought Kim.

As the miles raced by, she wondered about the villa. Could it be so dangerous? Was it in a parlous state of ruin, or was it dramatically perched over some perilous ravine? Was it slowly sinking into the mire of some unfathomable swamp? Was it right next to some revolting pig farm so that it reeked to high heaven? She couldn't wait to find out. The beautiful Italian countryside rolled by as she pondered these possibilities..

A villa sprung into view, and a sharp veer onto the road leading to it identified it as their destination. The reality was not any of the things Kim had imagined. The villa was an exquisite, picturesque monument to Italian style. It sat in its manicured grounds as if it had been painted there. Kim gawped at the beauty of the trees, well-tended gardens, and the elegant dwelling itself.

"Wow! You live here?" Kim gasped.

"You like? Yours for today. You're very welcome to my humble abode" smirked Svetlana.

They enjoyed a cold juice followed by a refreshing glass of prosecco – now becoming Kim's favourite. Kim was given a tour of the house, and marveled at it all.

They went out to sit around the pool, soaking up the brightening sunshine.

"I swim now" Svetlana stated, and she went inside and rapidly reappeared in her almost there bikini. She could be a model, mused Kim, regarding her slender frame silhouetted by the sunlight reflecting off the pool.

"You swim now?" invited the host.

"Yes" Kim mumbled, and she slipped inside and sought her bikini, now regretting bringing it.

They entered the water, which Kim found surprisingly cool, and after a few rapid lengths Kim hauled herself out. Svetlana laughed.

"Tired so soon – or saving your strength?" she grinned.

"Just a bit cool" Kim explained.

Svetlana slipped effortlessly out of the pool, and reached for a towel.

"Let me dry you" and Svetlana began to rub her tenderly with the towel. Suddenly Kim felt a little uncomfortable.

"You warming up? I warm you up nice and good, yes?" Svetlana queried and she smiled sweetly, her eyes peering into Kim's.

It finally dawned on Kim. The situation in which she now found herself was entirely of her own making. She simply had not grasped the multiple warnings provided. She desperately sought some escape from her awkward predicament. Her fertile imagination came to her rescue.

"Look" Kim ventured, "in Manchester we don't shilly shally around. If we fancy someone we get right to it. Then we have some chips and gravy, and once they're down, we get right to it again. So get some chips on cooking, and let's get to it!"

Svetlana was startled. "This is Europe! Here we are civilized! Love is not accompanied by chips and gravy!"

"There's never one without the other, so it's chips or it's nothing!" Kim railed.

"You're quite vulgar!" snapped Svetlana coldly. "It's out of the question now! Get dressed, I take you back where you belong!" and she stormed off, enraged.

Kim sighed a deep breath of relief, and calmly donned her attire.

*****

On the way back not a single word was exchanged. This suited Kim fine. Svetlana drove at a more moderate pace, and Kim relaxed and enjoyed the landscape flashing by.

At the hotel, the car stopped, Kim alighted, closed the door, and before she could utter any brief thanks Svetlana sped away.

*****

The next morning Kim had a routine pick up from the airport, and trailed around the concourse collecting her clients, marshalled them into the coach, before dropping them all off at their respective hotels. It was not a challenging task, but time consuming and not particularly interesting. There really was no scope for invention or amusement.

When she arrived back at her room, a bouquet of flowers had been left at her door. She opened the card mystified, and read the simple message: Sorry, Svetlana.

She found a receptacle to display the flowers and smiled to herself. Could have been worse, she thought.

*****

Later in the day, as she crossed the hotel patio, chatting to clients as she went, she spied Svetlana sitting alone at a table, sipping a drink and relaxing in the sun. She would have sidled away, but their eyes had met immediately, so having been spotted that option was gone. She smiled, and Svetlana beckoned her over. Kim slumped clumsily into the seat indicated.

"Thanks for the flowers, but really there was no need" Kim began.

"Look, I get it, we're from different backgrounds and countries, but we are in same boat" Svetlana announced.

Kim listened attentively as she went on.

"You must be as alone as I, for there are no gay bars in this region, let alone this little town. Chances of meeting someone almost nil" she stated.

Kim still listened carefully.

"So I say you have not had sex since you arrived, yes?" Svetlana hazarded.

"Very true" responded Kim somewhat taken aback, "not since I broke up from my last lover in England" she added – also true. Dave had been a nice lad, though a bit rough around the edges.

"But we can be friends, yes?" Svetlana suggested.

It occurred to Kim that Svetlana was intensely lonely – literally no one to converse or relax with, never mind anything else. A sense of sadness and empathy for her predicament swelled in Kim's heart. She reached out to where Svetlana's hand was resting on the table, and clasping it in both of her own hands, squeezed it.

"Yes, of course, love to. Worst of lovers, but best of friends" Kim replied tenderly.

"I let you share my juice" and Svetlana smiled as she poured out a glass for Kim.

"Thanks" mumbled Kim, "but if it's okay with you, we keep our friendship confidential – just between us".

"My sentiments exactly" agreed Svetlana, "your colleagues are such hard work as it is. No need for complications".

They sat sipping and chatting for a few minutes. Then Kim had a great idea.

"How would you like a walking tour of the old town of Garda?" she breathlessly suggested.

"I have done it many times, as tour guide, so thanks, but no thanks" Svetlana smartly riposted.

"Not with me you haven't. You don't know all the intricacies of the real history of the place – all the awful goings on over the centuries, and the horrors hidden within the ancient walls" she gushed.

Svetlana regarded her anew.

"So, you're going to teach me all about it, when I so carefully wrote the latest script, verified for both relevant interest and historical accuracy?" she mocked.

"Absolutely!" Kim exclaimed.

"Okay. I learn quick. I check your version later for facts" she warned and Svetlana drained her glass, arose, taking good care to strike an elegant pose, before leading Kim out of the hotel.

*****

They meandered along the prescribed route, and Kim churlishly pointed out various minutiae of architectural merit. She laboriously intoned a catalogue of dull facts and figures, while correctly identifying the crumbling monuments to which they related. Kim followed Svetlana's original rigid script for as long as she could bear it. Svetlana was deeply unimpressed. As they whirled around the corner bringing into sight Kim's favourite haunt, she leapt into top gear. Fable followed fable, each worse than its predecessor in its attention to gory detail and reckless carnage.

Svetlana objected strenuously to the first couple of tales.

"That's not true!" she yelped.

"That's even less true!" she observed.

Kim soldiered on defiantly, with a torrid tale of infidelity.

"I hope you don't subject our clients to this torrent of lies!" Svetlana railed.

"Course!" Kim gleefully admitted, "they love it!"

"No! Surely not!" and Svetlana cringed at the thought, but a grin developed on her lips.

As Kim worked her way along the pretty quaint lane, identifying each picturesque dwelling by referring to the horrors conducted within its confines, Svetlana started to laugh.

"It's not true!" she managed to utter between guffaws.

She laughed and laughed, staggering down the street, tears running from her eyes, as she absorbed the unlikely crimes and ruinous misconduct of the former inhabitants.

"This is not history, this is some sort of ghoulish, impure entertainment!" Svetlana pronounced as they arrived in the final square by the lakeside.

"Exactly!" agreed Kim, "Now you get it!".

Svetlana selected a café table at the water's edge, slipped daintily into a seat, and summoned a waiter. Kim seated herself beside her with barely a stumble or two.

"Due café latte, per favore" Kim addressed the waiter. He

noted the order and retreated from whence he had emerged.

"Brava!" Svetlana cheered. "So very well done! But I think I'm going to need a stronger drink to follow all that" she added.

"Punters usually go for gin" suggested Kim.

"Gin? Then so shall we" Svetlana chimed.

They sat in the shade, gazing over the shimmering lake, watching the brightly coloured boats come and go, enjoying the sight of the throng of holidaymakers ambling past, while steadily imbibing gin and tonics. Kim sipped; Svetlana quaffed as if it were wine. They chatted very easily. She is good company, thought Kim.

As the reddening sun slowly set over the lake, they lurched along the lake front seeking a building that resembled a hotel.

Several were spotted, but Kim was adamant that they were not her own. Svetlana made little contribution to the quest, other than remaining broadly upright. It was evident that Svetlana could not drive home – she probably would have had trouble identifying her own car. Kim hauled her into the hotel once it had been found.

"So now what?" she asked Svetlana as soon as they were securely in the lobby, but Svetlana merely smiled sweetly and swayed alarmingly. Kim headed for the lift, and maneuvered her cargo into it. A steady drift along the corridor, a brief fumble with her key, and her load was duly cast onto the Emperor size bed. Kim removed Svetlana's offending shoes, and somehow dragged her into what appeared to be a comfortable position.

Svetlana cried aloud "No, no, no more gin for me!" and said nothing else until dawn.

Kim crept into bed herself, and as she was drifting off into slumber, it crossed her mind she was now both a pretend daughter, and a pretend dyke. But things come in threes, she reasoned, so what shall I pretend to be next? After a few minutes of deep contemplation, she decided a pretend pop star would be excellent. While attempting to figure out how this might be accomplished, she fell asleep.

*****

Kim was awoken sharply by Svetlana's announcement.

"What?" Kim asked, sitting up in bed.

"Best day ever" Svetlana repeated.

Kim looked at her through bleary eyes. Svetlana was dressed, well groomed, and smiling brightly and cheerfully. And, as usual, immaculate in both her appearance and posture.

"So nice of you to let me sleep over" she remarked.

"Thank you" she added.

"That's what friends are for" Kim uttered in a voice so deep she was not sure it was her own. She coughed to clear her throat.

"I will let you be now. But we must repeat, very soon" and Svetlana blew a kiss as she let herself out.

Kim glanced at her phone, noted the early hour, and slumped back into bed. A thought struck her. Just slept with a lesbian. Can cross that one off my to do list, and that thought really tickled her pink. She chuckled merrily to herself as she dozed off back to sleep.

6 LIMONE

The brakes of the luxury coach screeched as the driver pulled up outside the hotel. Kim shepherded her flock into its interior, checking off the names on her clipboard. She smiled at Mrs. Ackroyd as she boarded, noting her outfit.

"Wow! Now that is all lemon, you weren't kidding! But it all looks great" complemented Kim. "Love the wide brimmed sunhat, too!"

"Many thanks – not quite my taste really – but one must indulge one's spouse occasionally" she whispered as she boarded.

Kim had spent hours studying the script for the tour, and was confident she could deliver it without resorting to fabrication. In any case, there were sufficient historical felonies to render embellishment unnecessary.

The route took them south from Garda, through Bardolino, skirting Lazise, and around the southern end of the lake, and then northwards again up the western shore to Limone. Along the way there way numerous small ports and villages to admire. A brief stop at Sirmione served as a refreshment break. Once the coach had rolled to a stop, and it was safe to stand, Kim lifted the microphone, and announced importantly "We have now left Veneto, and entered Lombardy".

Her attentive audience was not impressed. She went on and told them of the local attractions.

"At the end of the peninsula are the ruins of the villa of Caractacus….." but she was interrupted by laughter.

"Can't be Caractacus – he was a true Brit" one yelled out.

"Bet Caractacus is dancing in his grave now we're leaving the EU" another jibed.

"Catallus" intervened the driver.

"Oh, Catallus" corrected Kim, "now only a one hour stop here, okay?"

They all groaned and slowly disembarked. After a swift drink and brief stroll around, some of the intrepid explorers returned to their bus, preferring its shade to the crowded streets, roasting in the noonday sun. Others, including Kim, took a short boat ride out into the lake. The boatman explained that a volcanic spring lay below the lake, and hot water issued from it, right up to the surface of the lake. Kim laughed. This was too much like one of her own unlikely fables.

A bubbling area of the lake came into view, together with a distinct aroma of Sulphur. The boatman silenced his motor, and the boat glided into the froth. As directed they touched the water surface to find it quite hot. Kim yelped with delight – a fable come true! The boatman urged haste, as a queue of more boats was forming nearby. He swiftly brought them back to shore, and embarked his next load of disbelieving customers.

A stroll around the quaint square revealed a little café, where Kim and her charges managed to obtain a quick drink.

Once all were duly aboard the bus and carefully counted they settled down for the long drive along the lakeside to Limone. Kim provided occasional enlightenment along the way.

"And if you look at the grey tall villa on the right, by the lakeshore, this is the former residence of the famous opera singer Mussolini...." laughter again interrupted her delivery.

"He had a big gob but it wasn't for singing" someone yelled out. More laughter.

"More like choppin' than Chopin" quipped another.

"Anyway, that's where he lived" concluded Kim sharply. Must double check on that point she noted to herself.

"It is now a luxury hotel, over three thousand euros a night" she dutifully reported.

"They should've pulled it down" Mr. Ackroyd called out.

"Really, Arthur!" chided Mrs. Ackroyd.

The sun shone, and the engine droned, and Kim tried to provide some distraction, but without too much droning from herself. The hours soon slipped by – after all, it was a delightful journey. The coach halted at the waterfront coach park in Limone, and Kim called out the drill instructions.

"We meet here in two hours – no lingerers – please, we can't wait, so let's synchronize watches - three ten precisely – by my watch anyway" Kim mumbled into the microphone.

"Do we have to swim back if we miss the charabang?" queried one old gent.

"Most definitely" answered Kim, "so no tardiness!"

"Oh 'ell" he gasped, "better be nippy on me pins then".

They all clambered out, and dispersed to the various cafés and restaurants for some more well-deserved refreshments.

Kim smiled at the driver, and ambled down to the waterfront, slipped off her shoes, and sat on a low wall, dipping her feet in the cool water, sipping from her water bottle. She left the charms of the quaint old village for her charges to discover for themselves.

*****

After the prescribed two hours, the tourists reappeared at the coach, in dribs and drabs, until it seemed all were aboard. Kim began her essential headcount, which being satisfactory, she signaled to the driver to go. She double checked again by wandering up and down the aisle, verifying her first count. All was well, and away they went.

She noted Mrs. Ackroyd's wide brimmed sunhat once more, which she kept on her head for much of the return journey.

But something niggled at the back of Kim's mind.

She turned around and regarded all her charges. Some were dozing, other gazing out the windows, others chatting quietly among themselves.

But something was amiss.

Alarmed, Kim strode purposefully up and down the aisle again, pretending to count but examining each client carefully, to ensure that none were ill.

Then it struck her.

Mr. and Mrs. Ackroyd were chatting animatedly, and smiled as she went past, but this Mrs. Ackroyd was not the same Mrs. Ackroyd who had alighted in Limone.

Same hat, dress, shoes and bag, all lemon – exactly as

before, but the lady occupying the garish outfit was different. Kim stared, but had to look away, as she felt baffled and completely stupid. She sat down in her own seat at the front, but after a few minutes once again ventured along the aisle. She slipped into a vacant seat, and gazed nonchalantly out of the window, but listened carefully to the Ackroyds' discourse.

Mr. Ackroyd was explaining their new domestic arrangements to another day tripper.

"Only five hundred yards from the beach, isn't it Gladys?" he yelped with delight.

"And we'll soon make new friends there, won't we Arthur?" the current Mrs. Ackroyd added.

Kim glanced over. The hair was different, the poise, the voice, the gesticulations, the way she slumped in her seat – the real Mrs. Ackroyd had sat up straight. Kim was convinced. This was a fake Gladys Ackroyd. So what had become of the real Mrs. Ackroyd? Kim reflected on all the gory tales she had told. Was one of them now coming true?

*****

There were no stops along the way on the return journey. It felt like an interminable nightmare to Kim. She was glad when the hotel slipped into sight, and could barely wait to get back into it.

The coach roared away leaving in its wake an unwelcome belch of fumes. Kim watched her charges troop into the hotel, smiling and thanking them as they passed, while regarding the fake Gladys Ackroyd with barely disguised suspicion. None of the other travellers had noticed the difference, and once again she now doubted her concerns. Was she imagining it?

She carefully observed the Ackroyds waiting for the lift, and how the fake Gladys slithered along as she entered. Now she was again certain – this was a different woman. She resolved to do something about it. Quite what, she knew not.

She returned to her own room, flung open the windows, and drew a deep breath. She paced up and down, struggling to fathom some course of action. She glanced at her reflection in the mirror – duty calls she decided.

She picked up her phone and texted her colleagues 'emergency meeting ranch 9pm Kim' and set her phone down gently with a sigh. The die was now cast.

*****

Kim now paced agitatedly around the office awaiting her colleagues. They were prompt, and at nine on the dot were all seated at the table.

"Well?" Sara demanded.

They waited with baited breath.

"I lost one of my ladies in Limone" Kim began.

"What?" screeched Sara "You didn't count or wait?" she fumed.

"No, no, I did count" Kim explained, "the count was correct. But one of the ladies was a fake – not the same lady who got off the bus. Same outfit, different lady" she added.

"Explain yourself, clearly" Sara requested coldly.

Kim went through the whole saga, in glorious detail and in glorious technicolor. She worried that she feared the worst – a dead body would soon be discovered in Limone.

They all listened attentively and then relaxed.

"You idiot" muttered Rachel.

"Dozy git" mumbled Griff.

"You poor thing" sympathized Alice.

Kim awaited Sara's response. Sara's response took some time to erupt as her tension boiled into an explosion.

"Kim!" she balled, "Fantasies. Horrors. Nightmares. Desist!" and she banged the table so hard the room shook.

"This is the third time I've told you about this, and it's definitely the last! Daddy's girl or no daddy's girl - final warning!" she shouted, and kicked her chair back before leaping up menacingly and storming out.

"Out of order, Kim, well out of order" advised Griff, following Sara out.

Kim felt humiliated and sat silently.

"Look, sunshine," began Rachel "you're new to this, so it's no surprise you've got confused. But when people arrive on holiday – they're all tense and grouchy – and usually quite tired from the flight. Then after a few days, they relax, and start to enjoy themselves. They let their hair down, become more friendly and chatty. They really can seem like different people, and in a way, they are. You just get used to seeing it. Sometimes the transformation can seem quite remarkable – but that's all it is, same person, just in a different mood and with a refreshed outlook. We've seen it hundreds of times, so don't panic. Okay? And stop worrying!"

Rachel squeezed Kim's hand in reassurance.

"But it's not her" Kim doggedly insisted.

"Okay" Rachel conceded, "let's say it's not. I'll check for you".

She reached for her phone, and selected the speed dial number for the hotel.

"Hello, may I speak to your guest, Mr. Ackroyd?" she sweetly enquired.

After a pause, she continued.

"Mr. Ackroyd? It's Rachel, Tomlinson rep. Why, yes, we did meet in Verona!"

"I'm very well, thanks"

"Just wondered if everything was going well with your holiday?"

"All fine – oh good. And how was your trip to Limone?"

"That's great to hear. Would it be possible to have a word with Mrs. Ackroyd? Thanks".

"Mrs. Ackroyd – just wondering if your trip went okay today?"

"Good. And how was your guide, Kim? It was her first time to Limone".

"Really? Caractacus? Yes, I bet you all laughed. And you enjoyed the joke about Mussolini? Well that's great to hear. Anything else I can help you with?"

"So I hope you enjoy the rest of your holiday. Bye, thanks" and Rachel put down her mobile.

Rachel now turned on Kim.

"Sirmione and Mussolini's villa are on the way out to Limone – aren't they?" Rachel stated.

"Yes" admitted Kim.

"And that lady heard your blunders at those places – didn't she?" Rachel argued logically.

"Obviously" Kim uttered meekly.

"So it must be the same lady" Rachel reasoned.

"I suppose" Kim caved in.

"And don't joke about Mussolini – it's still a very raw point in Italy – okay?" Rachel advised.

"Okay" agreed Kim.

Rachel softened her tone. "Look, we all make mistakes. So just get over it".

"Okay" muttered Kim.

"Right. I'm off then. Bye" and Rachel left.

Kim and Alice remained seated at the table. Kim hung her head, avoiding Alice's stare.

"You're just not convinced, are you?" Alice enquired cautiously.

Kim faced her. "It was a different lady. I mean, we are wearing the same uniform, we are young women, broadly alike, but we are different people. No one who knows us two could mistake us, one for the other. But passing through a crowd, one could switch for the other, and no one might spot the difference".

"And you think that's what happened?" Alice replied.

"Yes, it did. The more I think about it, the more sense the plan makes. They sell their house in one town, go on holiday, and return to a new house in a new town where no one knows them. Who would know the Mrs. Ackroyd as presented wasn't the genuine one?" Kim argued.

"And unusually Mr. Ackroyd bought Mrs. Ackroyd a striking outfit, a blazing one that no one could miss, and an identical one for the substitute. Everyone sees the outfit, and not the lady wearing it" Kim reasoned.

"Sooner or later, a body is found in Limone, with nothing to identify it, and no one has ever been reported missing. The case goes unsolved, forever".

"And Mr. Ackroyd gets away with murder" Alice observed.

"Exactly" Kim cried.

"Okay, so what can I do to help?" asked Alice.

"Can you cover for me tomorrow, swap your day off – then I can investigate myself?" Kim pleaded.

"Okay, that's agreed. And then you can play detective" Alice quipped.

So there's my third pretence thought Kim, now I'm a pretend detective too.

7 THE SEARCH

Kim arose early, having decided upon a plan of action. She readied herself hurriedly, and headed down to the harbour area, and bought a ticket to Limone. She selected the Rapido service, which would get her there relatively quickly.

She was ashamed to admit to herself that she entirely enjoyed the journey there, but was glad though filled with trepidation as Limone progressively crept into sight.

She disembarked along a creaking gangplank behind a huge crowd, whom she found quite irritating. Did they not know she was a girl on a mission?

They did not. So they blocked her way and her view of the harbour area and its linked square at every available opportunity. Kim seethed silently.

There was no great police presence, or cordoned off areas, so clearly no dastardly crime had been discovered.

She reasoned that it would be impossible to dispose of a body amongst such a heaving mass of tourists, so Mr. Ackroyd must have led his prey somewhere around the edge of town, out of sight. They were on foot, and only two hours from start to finish would have been available to him.

Kim headed south, and searched around the shrub growth at the town limits. She systematically worked her way around the western perimeter of the of the built up area.

She found nothing of interest.

Disheartened and drenched with sweat, she took a coffee break in one of the charming cafés overlooking a delightful square. What a place to carry out an evil plot she thought to herself.

If only she spoke Italian, she could have asked a local where was there a handy spot nearby that would do for dumping a corpse?

The grim jest made her smile, but the harsh reality of what she was doing brought her train of thought up sharply.

She plodded on with her task, swinging around the western edge of the village, venturing up street after street, and eventually reaching the northern limits, but to no avail. She knew they could not have gone far, but she felt she had now covered all the possible out of sight points that would have served Mr. Ackroyd's grim task.

Exhausted and frustrated, she boarded the Rapido for the return trip. The lake surface frothed by as she pondered her next actions. She texted Alice to get any ideas from her.

*****

Alice met her on the quayside.

"Any joy?" she asked.

"Not a thing" moaned Kim, "not a wretched thing. One good point at least, no corpse has been discovered, there was no police activity at all".

"So will you call them now?" Alice queried "That's what I'd do. Report what you know, and let them investigate it all. It's their job when all said and done".

"I suppose you're right. Probably should have done that first anyway" Kim accepted the suggestion.

"Cop shop's about a couple of hundred yards north, along the main road from the bus station" Alice helpfully advised.

"Too tired now, I'll go first thing in the morning" Kim said. "And thanks for today, Alice" she added.

"No probs. See you then" and Alice went on her way.

Kim strolled along the promenade, thinking about the day's events. Or lack of events. It occurred to her that if Mrs. Ackroyd was still alive, every minute might count. With this dreary thought in mind, she made her way promptly to the police station as Alice had directed.

She stumbled reluctantly into its clinically cold entrance.

A startled policeman sat up.

"Buena Sera" he muttered.

"Hello" began Kim, and she related her tale in outline in the first instance.

The policeman nodded occasionally, listening attentively.

He then pulled out his mobile phone, tapped on it several times, and then typed carefully and slowly. He pressed an icon, and showed the screen to Kim.

It read "What do you want?"

He indicated the text keyboard displayed beneath this message, and lay the phone down flat on his desk so she could type into it.

She typed a short phrase. "I lost a lady in Limone, yesterday".

The gallant officer of the law pressed his icon, and the translation appeared in Italian. He read it, considered it for a moment and then steadily composed his response. He pressed his icon once more.

"Not a local police matter. Contact state police".

Kim absorbed the missive.

He put his phone away with a wild flourish and a resounding "Arrivederci!", and clearly the interview was concluded.

Kim retreated to the outside world, and drew a breath of fresh air. She made her way slowly back to the hotel, and once in her room was overwhelmed by a profound sense of gloom and foreboding.

Room service beckoned, and she ordered a large meal and opened a bottle of prosecco. As she ate she wondered how Mrs. Ackroyd was faring, assuming she was still alive.

She felt there was no more to be done that night, but then reached for her phone, connected to the wifi, and established the phone number of the nearest state police station. She jotted the number down, a task for tomorrow she decided, and then wearily readied herself for bed.

*****

Kim awoke somewhat later than normal, as it was her own day off. Once she was showered and dressed, she braced herself for the daunting task before her. She took a deep breath, and dialed the state police.

The phone rang for a considerable while, prior to

reverting to an answering machine, which then yielded a bewildering whirlwind of Italian, followed by the usual familiar beeps.

Kim was unprepared for this, and slammed the phone down. She collected her thoughts, jotted down a few notes, and went through a brief script in her mind.

She took a deep breath, and dialed again.

"Prego!" answered a voice immediately.

Kim was unprepared for this, and slammed the phone down once more.

"Oh for crying out loud, help me!" she yelled aloud.

"What help you need?" asked the hotel maid who had silently entered.

Kim jumped, completely startled.

"Sorry, should have knocked louder" apologized the intruder.

Kim smiled to reassure her. "No worries. Just trying to get through on a phone call".

"Okay. You busy. I come back later" and she scurried out.

Kim stood up, flexed her arms, strode purposefully around the room, took several deep breaths, and braced herself again.

"Once more into the breach, dear Kim!" she cried, and dialed again.

The phone rang for a long time, then switched to its automatic answer. Kim listened to the recorded torrent, and waited for the beeps, which never arrived. She was not sure whether or not to begin her sorry tale, and hesitated, waiting for the prompt.

"Prego!" yelled a human responder.

"Oh! Hello!" squeaked Kim. "Are you there?"

"Prego!" replied the dutiful servant of the law.

"Do you speak English?" Kim asked hopefully.

"Not anymore" was the unlikely reply.

Kim had to think what this meant. Was this a churlish refusal in the light of Brexit?

"Not since school" explained the officer.

"Only a bit now" he extended.

"I want to report a missing person" Kim ventured.

"Okay. You come to station. You file report" he instructed her.

"Peshiera del Garda" and he detailed the address. Kim wrote hastily.

"And is that near Garda?" Kim hopefully enquired.

"Bus one hour from Garda" was the reply.

"Okay, thanks, see you soon" and she ended the call.

*****

The bus ride was uneventful, and Kim sat back and relaxed, at least I'm doing something about it now she mused.

She actually enjoyed the journey this time. She had travelled this road only the day before, but had been working then. So much more fun as a passenger.

She alighted at the depot, and with help from her mobile, found her way to the state police station. More like an outpost, really, thought Kim.

She marched inside, expecting a posse of keen officers to be waiting with bated breath. It was not to be. Three policemen were present, one busy on the phone, the other two busy arguing with each other.

It was a dramatic and heated argument, which decayed into a sulky silence for a few minutes, but then flared up with renewed bitterness. None of them took a blind bit of notice of her. She waited impatiently, as the minutes rolled by. Finally, the man on the phone finished his call, signaled to her that she should take a seat, and then be began to write his report on the matter recently concluded on the phone. The other two blazed at each other. Kim feared it would end in fisticuffs, she watched, quite fascinated.

Eventually the third policeman approached her.

"Prego" he volunteered in a matter of fact way. She recognized his voice as the man to whom she spoke earlier.

"I would like to report a missing person" she breathlessly announced.

He wandered off to the back of the room, dodging around his warring colleagues, and rifled through a wad of forms. Satisfied he had retrieved the appropriate one, he maneuvered past the sparring two, and handed it to Kim.

"Complete!" he indicated. "All details, then sign here" and he indicated again. He proffered a pen, which Kim gratefully accepted.

She settled down to her penmanship, writing reams of information about herself in the requisite boxes. Then she attempted the same for Mrs. Ackroyd. Of course she knew precious little, once it was required to be stated in black and white. It was hard to think with the din from the pair of combatant officers, who had entered into a particularly fractious discourse with a distinct tone of venom. She attempted to relate the circumstances of her last sighting, and her cause for concern. It seemed a forlorn task.

Finally she handed the completed form to the policeman. He glanced at it, checking it was signed, then date stamped it with a loud clang, and lastly wrote a long number on the form. He separated a carbon copy, and gave it to her.

He pulled out his mobile phone, tapped upon it, keyed in some text, tapped an icon, and showed her the screen. Kim was not amused.

"Your crime number" it read, and he pointed to her copy of the form.

He now reached for a diary, and leafing through its pages, jotted a note in it. He turned once more to his phone.

Kim read the text as directed.

"Return here for interview" she learnt.

He pointed at the calendar, indicating a date in over three weeks' time. Kim duly recorded the date, and left without even wishing him any thanks.

As she stepped outside, it was good to be back in the brilliant sunshine, out from the austere gloom, and away from the incessant racket raised by the quarrelling coppers.

No hope for Mrs. Ackroyd there, she concluded, dumping the carbon copy form in the first litter bin she came across. She desperately needed a drink, and having found a decent café, decided an ice cream would help too.

*****

The bus ride back to Garda was a solemn affair. There seemed to be no more she could do. Only Rachel was fluent in Italian, and she had made it perfectly plain that she would not help. Alice was willing, but could do little to assist.

Svetlana – what about Svetlana? She had boasted of her linguistic skills. And she was in charge, above Sara too. Mrs. Ackroyd was just as much her responsibility as my own, Kim realized.

Back in Garda, she made her way directly to the Ranch, and let herself into the office, and rummaged around until she found Svetlana's number.

Again she prepared herself for a difficult conversation.

She paused before dialling. "Oh what the hell" she called out loud, and dialled.

It rang for a moment, then she heard Svetlana's voice faintly, against a considerable background noise.

"Prego" Svetlana said.

"It's Kim" she began.

"I'm in car. I call you back soon. Ciao!" and the line went dead.

Kim put the phone down wearily. She waited, but no call

was returned. After an hour, she locked up the office, and slowly made her way back to her room.

She entered, opened the windows wide, leaned on the rail and stared out at the view.

"Does nobody listen?" She lamented aloud.

She retreated to her bed and flung herself upon it.

After a short rest, she realized she needed a change of scene and maybe some company too. She made her way down to the hotel terrace, slumped into a chair at an empty table, and when the waiter appeared ordered a stiff drink, rules or no rules.

She sat sipping quietly, hoping one of her nearby clients might strike up a conversation, but none did. She felt that she did not have the energy to commence one herself.

Her phone finally rang.

"Prego!" she tried. It sounded convincing.

"Brava! Kim, you are almost fluent!" Svetlana mocked.

Kim laughed. "Oh, hi, look, Svetlana, I need your help and advice".

"Of course you do, I know this from the start" Svetlana replied.

"No, about a specific matter. It would be easier to talk to you in person, rather than on the phone" suggested Kim hopefully.

"Okay. Look behind you. I come over".

Kim turned around to see Svetlana gracefully arise from a seat at the far end of the terrace, and then sashay with a broad swagger down its whole length. Kim stared, fascinated. I don't think I could accomplish that swaying, rhythmic sashay she thought, nor would I have the confidence if I could. Many eyes followed Svetlana as she made her progress. Finally she slipped elegantly into the seat opposite Kim.

"So. What specific matter?" Svetlana enquired.

Kim explained the whole sorry tale to her. Svetlana listened carefully, never asking a question.

When Kim ended, Svetlana spoke.

"So. You and I are different. Yes? We see women in a different way. Yes? We really notice, because it is who we are. We really look at women. Yes? So you say this woman was not the same woman – then I believe you – because I know you really look at women too. Just now, I walk across here – you look at me. You watch my every move – you did didn't you? You can't help it, it's natural, I'm good looking, so you stare at me. It's okay, because I like to be admired".

Kim blushed scarlet.

Svetlana smirked. "I make you blush. How pretty! You make my day!"

Kim sipped her drink. "Well, at least you believe me. It's good that someone believes me at last".

"I do. So now what to do. The local police are hopeless, as you found out. You need the Carabinieri, the federal police, there is an office in Malcesine, just an hour up the shore".

"Great!" Kim enthusiastically responded. "Will you translate for me?"

"No, they will not accept a third party translator. They have their own translators, but, better still, I know that there is an English speaking officer based there".

"So no need for any translator?" Kim asked.

"Exactly. But I will drive you there now, so drink up!"

8 THE COMMISSARIO

Svetlana was as good as her word, and drove like a maniac along the highway by the lakeside. Kim wondered if they would end up being the subject of a police enquiry, attempting to establish the identities of the two bodies discovered in the wreckage of an Alfa Romeo stuck half way up a tree.

The car screeched to a halt outside the barracks.

"I won't wait for you, because you'll be all day in there" Svetlana warned.

Kim climbed out. "Thanks, Svetlana!" she called as the car swung around, and she just heard a sound resembling "Ciao!" as it swooped away.

Kim gingerly walked past the barriers and no entry warnings into the dark den of the Carabinieri.

An officer greeted her.

"Prego?" he asked.

"Hi, Do you speak English?" Kim ventured.

"Italiano!" he responded abruptly. "Commissario Sant Angelo, Englesi!" and he pointed to the clock.

Kim strained to understand. He pulled a chair over, stood on it, and pointed to four pm. Two hours away, thought Kim. He climbed down, carried the chair out into a corridor, and pointed to it, indicating that Kim should wait there. She meekly obeyed. He returned to his office and closed the door.

Bored senseless, she regarded her surroundings. A long corridor, painted grey, a bit stuffy and rather warm. Great way to spend a sunny afternoon. Several doors led off the corridor, presumably into offices, but there was an alcove, where a whirring sound and a periodic flashing light betrayed the presence of a busy photocopier. The interior of the alcove was just out of her line of sight. Now and then an officer or two would appear, enter the alcove, and emerge with wads of paper. Exciting stuff, thought Kim.

The minutes rolled away. A door at the very end of the corridor opened, and a beautiful woman entered. She had long black hair, a white blouse, tightly drawn, and a bright red skirt, also tightly fitted. Maybe she was in her mid-thirties, thought Kim. Needs to lose a few pounds, bit of a diet and some regular exercise is on the cards, she unkindly prescribed.

The woman emitted a "Ciao!" as she passed Kim, then tapped quietly on a door three times, paused, then once more, then finally once loudly, twice more gently, and once loudly. She then slipped into the photocopier alcove.

After a few minutes, the door thus signaled, opened, and a smartly uniformed policeman emerged, and vanished into the alcove also.

Kim could not see, but heard quite distinct sounds of kissing and fumbling. Her ears pricked up. Whispers in Italian were clearly discernable below the drone of the photocopier. There was a louder rustling of clothing, deep masculine grunts, and light feminine moans and whines. When the photocopier light flashed, shadows were cast on the wall within Kim's field of view. She was intrigued to see some quite novel postures adopted, if only in silhouette. First one, and then another; each was illuminated in turn. Of course, Kim paid mere incidental attention to these proceedings. This went on for quite some time, at least twenty minutes by Kim's watch, before the undeniable acoustic evidence of simultaneous orgasms was forthcoming. At least someone's getting it thought Kim. And that lady's had a refreshing stretch and plenty of quality exercise too. Three sessions a day would soon see her nice and trim, she concluded.

The woman emerged, and uttered a "Ciao!" as she swept past Kim. The policeman also emerged, and returned to his office. Good afternoon's work completed, Kim surmised.

At last a door opened, and a policeman beckoned her. She arose, and was shown through an outer office, and directed to enter an inner office.

She timidly stepped forward.

A uniformed officer was seated at his desk. He did not stand, or welcome her. She stared at him.

His thick hair was a deep black, his posture in his chair suggested a great height, his large hands, bulging arms and broad chest indicated a fine physique, and his blazing brown eyes were deep set in the most beautiful face she'd ever seen on a man. She simply gawped at him.

He knew he was good looking, and was quite accustomed to such admiration. He ignored it.

"How can I assist you?" he gently enquired, in a sonorous voice, and he indicated that Kim should sit in the chair provided.

Kim sat, but was at a loss for words.

"Perhaps we can start with your name?" he suggested.

Kim knew the answer to that one, for sure. Her mother had told her long ago, and more than on one occasion. If only she could just recall it.

"Shall I guess? You say when I get it right" he joked. "Elizabeth, Susan, Margaret...."

"Kim! It's Kim! I do know it! It's Kim!" she yelped in delight.

"Very good, Kim, so how can I assist you?" he repeated.

"Well" began Kim, and she then informed the attentive public servant of all the facts she knew, and the dark suspicions she harboured. He nodded sagely throughout. After some minutes thinking in silence, he advanced his conclusion.

"Nothing you have said proves that a substitution and an imposture has taken place. It hints, but does not prove. I fear that while what you have told me arouses my concern, I am not sure that on the strength of this alone I can take any action" he calmly ruled.

He went on. "You did not know this lady very well, and had only seen her a few times before, and only in passing. You had not spent much time with her. So after a nice lunch, and a stroll around a pretty harbour, she might well have relaxed, both physically and emotionally, so that she seemed like quite a different person. So you see, your colleagues' arguments do hold some merit".

Kim was visibly disappointed. She struggled to bring to mind any other snippets of information she may have missed. There must be something, she felt.

"Look," she argued, "however great Italian cuisine, and however brilliant Italian sunshine, and however picturesque an Italian harbour, the fact remains that it is not possible that in the short time of two hours a woman can lose six years in age, six pounds in weight, but gain six inches in height. It was not the same woman!"

Now this did strike a chord with the policeman. Never mind style, posture, gesticulations, he knew they could be changed. But age, weight, height, this was the stuff of policework.

"Right! I am convinced there is a case to investigate!" he bellowed at her. "So now you are a witness to a possible crime, or crimes. You now follow my instructions" he snapped at her.

She jumped, quite alarmed at his sudden outburst.

"Okay" she muttered.

"You will discuss this with no-one. Only me. You will conduct no further enquiry alone, or at all. You will not approach Mr. Ackroyd, or his suspected accomplice, or ask any questions of them. You just carry on, and do your own job as normal. If they speak to you, you give them no cause for concern, but chat as usual. Understand?" he asked.

"Yes, completely" Kim agreed.

"So now I go to Limone, to see for myself. You come too!" he added. "And then we shall see!" and he rose to his full height – Kim now saw that he was indeed a huge man. No messing with him, she thought.

*****

A driver was summoned, and he brought the car around, and Kim and the Commissario climbed in the back. The dutiful officer flipped the car onto the highway, and then drove wildly, on many occasions on the correct side of the road, siren blaring and lights flashing. This is more like it, thought Kim.

It was tremendous fun, speeding through red lights and around sharp bends with no consideration for oncoming traffic.

They skirted around the northern end of the lake, before heading south to Limone. The Commissario muttered some vague instruction, and the siren quieted and the lights quenched. The car advanced very slowly into Limone, and then crept into the centre of a pedestrianized square. Must get one of these, thought Kim. So convenient for so many outings.

They alighted, and the senior officer looked all around and smelt the air. He signalled for Kim to follow. She trailed behind him, but he waved for her to be at his side. They ambled around with no purpose that was obvious to Kim.

Finally he spoke. "What are your favourite flavours?" he enquired quietly.

Kim glanced at him. Was he serious?

"Well?" he asked.

"Chocolate, strawberry, and lemon" Kim responded, quite baffled.

"Excellent" he replied.

He then approached an ice cream stand, and ordered a large cone containing those flavours for her, and a large chocolate mint for himself. He handed her the cone, and started to enjoy his own. She followed suit. Actually, she thought, needed this, haven't had any refreshment for hours.

They ambled along some side streets to the edge of town.

"Everyone thinks a policeman eating an ice cream is not on duty, so they all relax, and then you can see more of what is actually going on" he explained.

Kim smiled. "That's clever".

"We look up this street, to the end" he stated, indicating a narrow lane.

"I already looked around at all the rough ground at the end of this road" Kim hesitated.

"We look again. Your thinking was right. We must check the nearby town boundaries, but we look together, quietly. Not a huge search with many police" he responded.

Nothing was seen, so they repeated the view on another street, and another. They advanced up a fourth steep lane, empty handed, as the ice cream was all gone.

"This is the one!" he called out. "I knew it was here somewhere".

Kim followed him up the incline. "I checked this one out, too" she objected.

"We keep going" he said.

They went on through the rough bushes and shrubs, and on to the clear ground beyond.

"There can't be anything further on" Kim stated, "which is why I stopped here".

"There can be and there is" he replied.

As they moved forward, a great pit came into view. It was twenty feet deep, twenty feet wide, and maybe sixty feet long. Its sides were quite vertical.

"Oh my God" cried Kim as she peered in. "It's enormous".

"I knew they were here somewhere" explained the chief.

"Is it old mine workings?" asked Kim.

"No. Old quarry, then later used for lemon trees. They grew the trees at the bottom. Hot in summer, and then covered the pit in winter to keep out the rain, wind and frost. The trees survived, and the valuable lemons went to market in Austria. All this area was in Austria, back then, and they didn't allow in cheap Italian lemons".

"Amazing it's still here, and not fenced round" Kim stated the obvious.

"We see the next one" and he led her onward. Another similar pit came into view, but that too was clear.

A third pit, even longer than the other two, came into sight. They peered into its depths. They leaned precariously over the edge to see immediately below the vertical drop. A bright lemon figure was clearly visible.

"That's Gladys Ackroyd!" screeched Kim, pointing at the prone body below.

The face of the Commissario blanched a pure white.

The body was lying with the head on the handbag, and the sunhat over the head. There was no sign of life. They edged around to one side, to get a better view, and to find a way down. There was no way down, or back up. The sides were vertical all around – a perfect trap.

The policeman called on his radio to his colleague in the car. A brief exchange followed. Then he pulled out his mobile, and made numerous calls. Kim understood none of this, but had no doubt of its content.

After half an hour the first sirens could be heard, and many more followed. Soon a host of firemen, policemen and ambulance paramedics were milling around the pit. The first fireman descended on a rope, and a paramedic followed. Others went down. First aid was administered.

"She's still alive – but only just" explained the Commissario to Kim.

"Thank God!" Kim wept.

A rig was set up, and a stretcher lowered, and the forlorn lady was hauled up, mask, oxygen tank, saline drip and stretcher all together. The whole package was bundled into an ambulance which wailed as it sped away. The rescue crew were saved from their duty at the bottom of the pit, and the site was taped off by the police.

"So, Kim. Well done!" congratulated her companion. "But your duty is not yet over. Paperwork. Lot's of it" he warned.

Kim groaned audibly.

"We return to my office. Normally I give this duty to a junior, but as only I speak English, I must do it myself" he added.

Could be worse, Kim mused. "Okay. Let's get on with it".

The same driver in the same car drove the same route in reverse order but the same manner back to Malcesine. Kim loved it.

*****

After the dreary process of completing the witness statements, enlivened only by coy glances at what she now considered to be her own private policeman, Kim was taken back to her hotel, in a moderately driven old police car.

She staggered into her room and flopped onto the bed. After a five minute respite, she called room service and ordered everything she could think of. She felt she deserved a substantial feast accompanied by an abundance of alcohol.

By the time she had eaten most of what had been provided, she began to relax and wind down. Her nerves tensed again as her phone rang.

"Hi" she answered.

"Well done, Kim," Svetlana's voice congratulated "I had a call from the Carabinieri, and they told me all about it. Amazing, so very well done. But they asked me to remind you not to say anything to anyone, especially the Ackroyds, or rather half of them plus the fake one. So tomorrow you have a day off, I will cover your roster. You just stay in your room, and keep out of sight, Okay?"

"Oh, that's brilliant, that's so good to know" she thanked. She felt so relieved.

"That is no problem at all. My duty at the very least. Keep in touch, ciao!" and Svetlana was gone.

Kim felt much more comfortable now she could indulge in some serious wine tasting. She set to her task with gusto, and the results were entirely satisfactory, a long and deep repose.

*****

The next day saw very little of Kim. She emerged from bed shortly before noon, and flung open her balcony doors to let in fresh air and some of the noonday sun. A long bath, and a quick room service lunch, set her up nicely for lounging on the balcony, watching the world go by. She felt really pleased with herself.

A knock at the door, broke her reverie. She opened it to find Alice in a state of alarm.

"Are you alright? Sara said you were off ill, and that Svetlana was covering your shift. I thought things must be serious to get her involved. You okay?" she gushed.

"I'm fine, come on in" and Kim showed her to the balcony. "Grab a seat and relax. I am just great".

"So did you have any joy with the police?" Alice gently enquired.

Kim was about to blurt out her actual good news, but recalled all the admonitions and warnings she'd had on the matter. So she invented some good news.

"The police are actively investigating now. They are very confident of resolving the mystery soon. So I am more than happy to leave it to them".

"That's great. We'll keep right out of it then" Alice suggested. "So what are you up to now?"

"I'm just chilling and enjoying a day off, courtesy of Svetlana".

After a brief pause, "What do you think of her?" Alice probed.

"Not sure yet. Still don't really know her that well" dissembled Kim.

"Take my advice and stay well away, she's weird. Okay boss though" Alice added.

*****

9 ARREST

Kim received and early morning call a couple of days later. It was Commissario Sant Angelo.

"Buongiorno" began the policeman. "Today we make the arrest, and I would like you to accompany me. I pick you up in half an hour – yes?"

"Right, fine" replied Kim nervously. "Anything....." but the call ended abruptly before she could ask.

Fine, thought Kim. She readied herself, and made her way down to the car park.

A police car swept into view not long after. A rear door opened, and she piled in. Mrs. Ackroyd was there, her arm in a sling.

"Mrs. Ackroyd!" yelped Kim, "Are you all right?"

"I am very well thank you, all things considered" she smiled graciously. "I believe I owe my life to you, a debt I can never repay. My most earnest thanks".

"How's your arm?" Kim enquired.

"Sore, but it will mend. Unlike my marriage, now beyond repair, I warrant" she answered.

"So what happened that day?" asked Kim.

"Well" began Mrs. Ackroyd, "we alighted from the bus

with everyone else, and strolled along, and selected a café and bought a cold drink. Then Arthur said he'd heard that a Harley Davidson motorbike had been abandoned in a pit somewhere nearby, and he would like to see if this was true. It might be very valuable. I laughed at the idea, but he persisted, so I condescended to indulge him, and we set off along a steep lane to view this wretched wreck. We came across one pit, and then another. Frankly I was losing my patience, but he said just one more to view, so we trudged across the rough ground, and then he yelped with delight as he spotted his blessed vintage motorbike. He pointed into the chasm, but I couldn't see it, so he suggested I needed to lean over to see as it was at the bottom of the face. I dutifully leaned, saw nothing, but felt an almighty shove which had me hurtling over the edge. That push could not have been delivered by himself, as he was to my left. Another miscreant must have been in hiding. I plunged down, thinking my last moments had come. I awoke, I don't know how much later, in pain, but able to stand. A muddy patch had broken my fall. I looked around, and saw that I was trapped. I screamed for help, until I was hoarse, but I was unanswered. My phone was missing from my bag. I had no drink. I thought I would perish. I did have a bottle of moisturizer, and I applied that liberally until it was gone, it helped cool me down. Night passed, the a whole day, without relief or rescue. Another night passed, I made peace with my maker, made myself comfortable, and laid down to die".

Kim's eyes filled with tears as these details, already imagined, were now brought to light. Even the Commissario, who had heard it several times, and written it all down, was affected once more.

"And now we make arrests" said the Commissario from the front seat. "Mr. Arthur Ackroyd and one other person still not identified" he added.

The car sped swiftly along the modern highway to Verona

airport, and pulled into a rear service area. They got out, and heavy doors were opened into the secure zones not seen by the public. Following a security officer's lead, they all trooped into a control room, where a field of screens displayed the various areas of the airport. They pored over the screens for some minutes.

"There's my errant husband!" pointed out Mrs. Ackroyd, "But I can't make out who that woman is with him".

"So now what?" asked Kim.

"We wait for them to go through passport control. My men are manning the desks this morning. See what name comes up as she goes through" explained the lawman.

They watched and waited, as the crowd milled around, and then it lurched forward as a gate number was displayed on the information screen. Their targets passed through. A side screen in the control room reported their names as Mr. and Mrs. Ackroyd.

"Good!" stated the Commissario. "That is proof of imposture" he intoned. "Now we go to greet them. Please stay behind me" he instructed.

They followed him as they made their way along spartan narrow corridors and undecorated stairwells. Finally they burst through a doorway, into the gate waiting area. The two were soon spotted amidst the tumult.

"I approach, you two stay close but behind me" directed the Commissario. They meekly obeyed. But Mr. Ackroyd recognized Kim.

"Kim!" he yelled, "come to see us off?"

Kim merely smiled.

"Your full name please?" asked the large policeman.

"Mr. Arthur Ackroyd" he responded truthfully.

"And yours?" the lawman enquired, looking directly at the lady.

"Mrs. Gladys Ackroyd" she responded untruthfully.

"Good" said the Commissario. He glanced at a woman standing a few yards away to his left, who was holding her bag up in a peculiar way. She nodded in assent.

"Excellent! All recorded." the Commissario concluded.

The real Mrs. Ackroyd now emerged from the milling throng.

"I'm Gladys Ackroyd! That's Tina, a cashier from the pound shop in Milton Keynes!" she screeched.

The two culprits froze in horror.

Mrs. Ackroyd had more to say. "Not even a cashier from John Lewis or Marks and Spencers! The pound shop! That just adds insult to injury!" and she glared at Mr. Ackroyd.

The lawman beckoned with his hand, and four officers grabbed the guilty pair from behind, and marched them away.

"Thanks for choosing Tomlinson Holidays, and be sure to fly Tomlinson Airlines on your release from prison many years hence!" quipped Kim as they were led off.

✳✳✳✳✳

On the way back, the Commissario explained his thinking.

"Hard to prove attempted murder; it would be your word against his, concerning the events in Limone that day. But now we can prove the imposture, the main charge follows that logically. Case closed" he stated.

As the car engine droned on their return journey, Kim finally relaxed.

"So what will you do now, Mrs. Ackroyd" Kim asked.

"Please, I would be honoured if you call me Gladys. I think you've earned it. And so what next? I shall go to my new home in Bournemouth, as planned. I shall make new friends, and a new life there, as planned. But without that brute. And I shall set up a guest room, for which you shall have a standing invitation, to stay as often and as long as you like" she exuded.

"Great, thanks" responded Kim.

"And once the conviction is secure, I shall seek a divorce, by way of employing a rottweiler of a lawyer, and ensure the whole home is solely in my name. I shall never see that creature again. I am also resolved to enjoy every single day allotted to me" she added.

"Now that sounds like a plan" Kim enthused.

Once they got back to Garda, Kim was dropped off at her hotel. She hugged Mrs. Ackroyd, and bade her farewell. The Commissario called out "Arrivederci" and the car sped away. Kim waved until it vanished from sight. Don't suppose I'll ever see him again she ruefully thought.

*****

10 AFTERMATH

Heroine or not, Kim had to go back to work. Work that now seemed at times a little dreary, but then when she thought about it, she could manage quite happily without so much excitement.

The usual weekly meeting came round, and the team assembled in the Ranch.

"Okay, we're all here so let's get on with it" opened Sara. "Kim, apologies due, so apologies given, and very well done in saving Mrs. Ackroyd".

"Yes, well done, sorry for not believing you" Rachel admitted.

"Yeah, nice one" Griff agreed.

"Knew you could" Alice chipped in.

"So very nice of you all" smirked Kim.

"There'll be a press announcement, and all that, and Svetlana will deal with that and all that sort of stuff, so Kim you just keep schtum, okay?" Sara explained.

"You bet" replied Kim, "I'm keeping a low profile from now on".

Sara went through the usual admin work, and closed the meeting in her normal style. "Meeting over!"

*****

Svetlana lived up to Sara's promise. She met the press, the local radio, and regional TV. She waxed lyrical in fluent Italian about how her team had saved the day, under her unstinting direction and unwavering eye for detail. Kim was never mentioned by name, and although she could not follow the details of the saga as presented, she caught hold of the general idea that Svetlana was the true heroine. And that suited her just fine. All she wanted now was a quiet life.

The true facts were not lost on the hierarchy of the Tomlinson Group. The chairman decided another visit to northern Italy was in order.

*****

Kim's mobile rang, and she heard the enquiry "Kim Tomlinson?"

She admitted to the fact. "Yup".

"This is the secretary to Lord Tomlinson" the voice advised. "Are you available for dinner tonight?"

"Yup" concluded Kim after a moment's consideration.

"Good. A car will pick you up at seven sharp. Good day" and the secretary was gone.

Suits me, thought Kim.

*****

She was ready and waiting outside the hotel at seven, dressed smartly if not glamourously.

A white Bentley convertible rolled almost silently into the car park. Its uniformed chauffeur got out, and opened a door for her.

"Miss Tomlinson?" he invited.

"Thank you" beamed Kim, entering as gracefully as she could muster. Wish I'd dressed up a bit fancier, she wistfully thought.

The car glided effortlessly into the hills and away from the lake. It cruised past some distinctly impressive private villas, before swinging into a driveway. At first sight Kim thought the building might be a villa, but as they approached see could make out that it was a small but exclusive hotel. Definitely not on the tourist trail, Kim decided.

She was led inside, and then out the rear to a small patio, where barely a dozen tables vied for space. At one table sat the formidable Lord Tomlinson. He rose to greet her.

"Miss Tomlinson, Lord Tomlinson, entirely at your service" he gleefully asserted.

"Thanks, nice to see you again, and pleased to be invited" Kim assured him.

"Do sit down. Champagne, I think, for our own local heroine. And for this occasion not the local imitation, I can't abide that prosecco, but the real thing" and he ordered just so.

"So, how was your ordeal? Are you quite recovered? Do tell me all about it" he excitedly asked.

She related the saga in its entirety, and the earl listened attentively, and laughed loudly at the antics of the local police.

"They really are almost hopeless" he ventured, "more like our traffic wardens, some of them. But the Carabinieri are a different kettle of fish. You need to be wary of them" he warned.

"Yes, I figured as much" replied Kim.

"Though of course you did have one advantage in your favour. You are after all, quite the practiced expert in imposture. Takes one to know one I suppose" he chided.

Kim laughed. "Well, yes. Sorry about that. I'll drop that charade quietly, somehow or other".

"As it happens that may not be in our best interest. I have been quite wallowing in the reflected glory of your achievement, and receiving congratulations from all and sundry regarding the rescue accomplished by my very own daughter" he explained.

"Oh. That's unexpected" Kim suggested.

"Indeed. The general rumour, I gather, is that you are an illegitimate daughter who has been squirrelled away for years, and that now you have emerged, you are making a name for yourself. Good breeding will out, I have been assured" and he waited for her response.

"Oh dear, this is getting to be a mess" Kim worried.

"Further, as I failed to immediately deny the connection, I am now enmeshed in the artifice just as much as you are. And the last time we met, I said I would have no part of it, yet here I am a party to the deception" he admitted.

"I see. Sorry about that" Kim repeated.

"So now I must invite you officially to be my fake, but illegitimate, daughter" he ventured.

Kim cried with laughter. "And I invite you to be my fake illegitimate father" she managed between guffaws.

"So that's agreed, I take it" he concluded.

"Yup" said Kim. "You know, I'm quite used to getting propositioned by drunken old men, but up until now I've always said no" she added helpfully.

He wept with laughter.

"In any case, my own daughter, while I am very proud of her, and love her dearly, and in spite of her numerous accomplishments and achievements, is in fact, as dull as dishwater. I haven't had a laugh with her, or any kind of merriment, for over a decade. And with you I laugh so easily. I wish you were my real daughter" he declared.

"That cannot be" Kim sighed. "Fake is all that's on offer".

"Then I'll take that offer. Perhaps we can meet up periodically?" he suggested.

"I would love that!" Kim exclaimed.

*****

Back at her hotel, Kim lay on her bed, turning all these events over in her mind.

Pretend daughter – check.
Pretend lesbian – check.
Pretend detective – check.

Now there's a merry threesome she concluded.

THE END

Printed in Great Britain
by Amazon